Mad About
Rockets, Stars, and outer space!

make believe ideas

Our galaxy

A **galaxy** is a huge space filled with billions of stars, dust, and gas. Our galaxy is called the **Milky Way**. It contains our entire **solar system**.

Mad about galaxies

The magnificent Milky Way is in the shape of a giant spiral.

There are over one hundred billion stars in the Milky Way— that's more than ten stars each for every person on the Earth!

Scientists think there are hundreds of billions of galaxies in the Universe. Maybe people just like us are living in them!

The Milky Way

On clear nights you can see the **Milky Way** from the Earth. It stretches across the sky like a misty, glowing band.

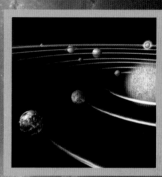

**Our solar
system is here!**

Solar system

The **solar system** started forming over four billion years ago! Today, it contains the Sun, moons, asteroids, comets, and all the planets, including our world, which is called **Earth**.

All the planets circle around the Sun in the same direction. The journey the planets make is called an **orbit**.

Mad about the solar system

There are eight planets in the solar system.

Pluto used to be the ninth planet, but in 2006 scientists decided that it was too small to count as a planet.

If you shouted in space, no-one would hear you. Even if they were standing next to you!

Planets

1 Mercury
2 Venus
3 Earth
4 Mars
5 Jupiter
6 Saturn
7 Uranus
8 Neptune

The Sun

The **Sun** is a massive **star** in the middle of our **solar system**. It gives us heat and light on Earth.

Mad about the Sun

Unlike the Earth, the Sun isn't solid. It's actually an enormous ball of gas.

The Sun acts like a gigantic anchor. It stops all the planets from flying off into space!

Without the Sun, nothing could live on Earth. Our planet would be completely frozen.

On its surface, the Sun is 250 times hotter than the Earth! Ouch!

Sunset

The **Earth** turns in a circle once a day. We see the **Sun** rise and set because the Earth is turning, not because the Sun is moving.

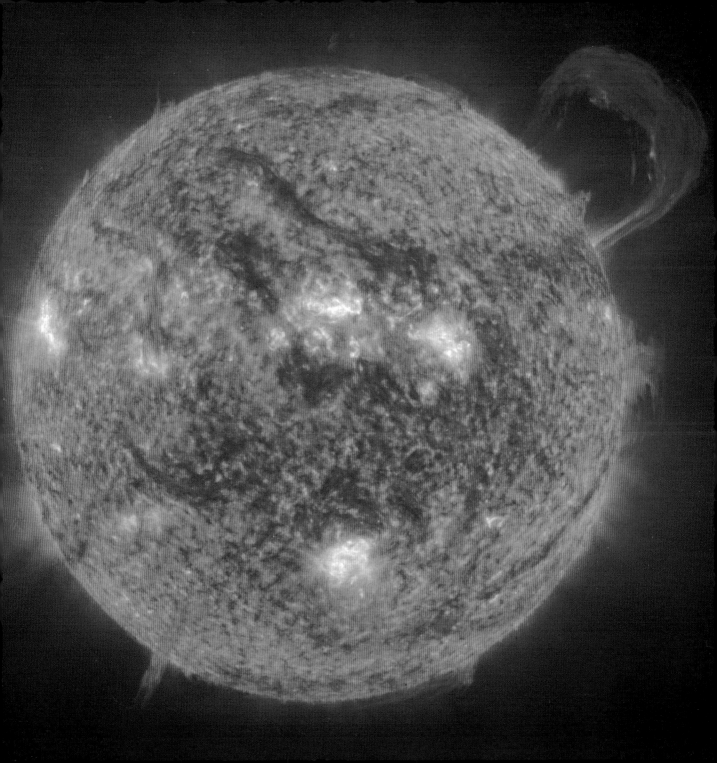

Rocky planets

The **rocky planets** are the four planets closest to the Sun: **Mercury**, **Venus**, **Earth**, and **Mars**. They are small in comparison to the other planets.

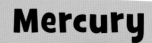
Mercury

Which is the biggest?

This diagram shows how big the other **rocky planets** are compared to the Earth.

Earth

Mercury   Venus   Earth   Mars

Mars

Venus

Mad about rocky planets

Speedy Mercury is the fastest planet. It can travel at 30 miles (48 km) per second! That means it would take just 13 minutes to travel around the Earth.

Sizzling Venus is the hottest of the planets. It's hot enough to cook a pizza!

Earth is our home planet. It takes a year for the Earth to circle around the Sun.

If you could drive through space it would take you over 66 years to reach Mars.

Outer space!

Use your stickers to make
a space scene!

Outer space!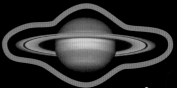

Use these stickers to complete your space scene!

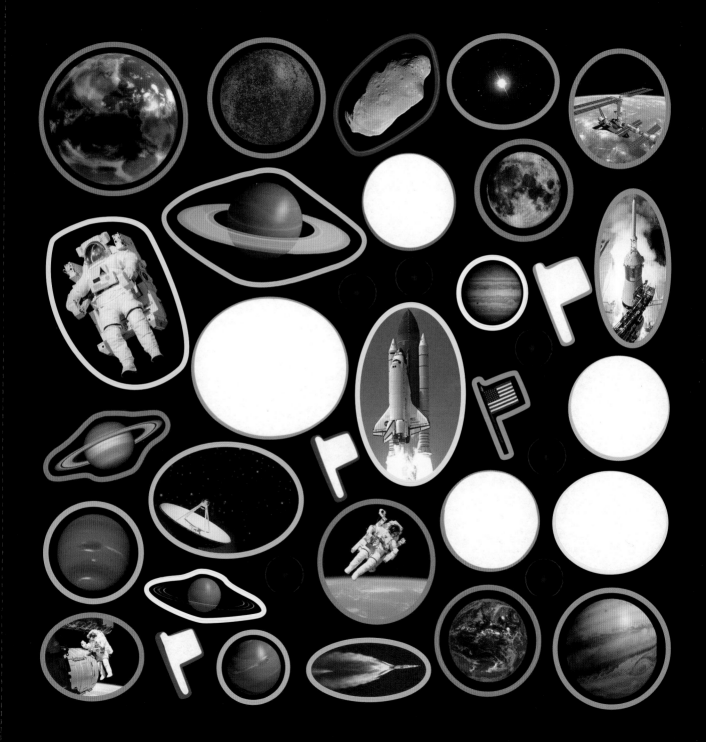

Gas planets

The **gas giants** are the four **planets** farthest away from the Sun: **Jupiter**, **Saturn**, **Uranus**, and **Neptune**. They are massive compared to the Earth!

Saturn

Which is the biggest?

This diagram shows how big the **gas planets** are compared to Earth.

Jupiter

Earth   Jupiter   Saturn   Uranus   Neptune

Saturn's rings are made of ice and rocks

rings......

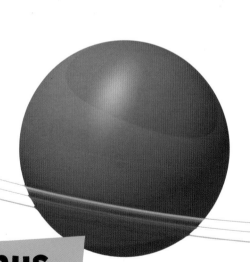

Jupiter is huge! It's the biggest planet in the solar system.

Saturn is the only planet that would float—if you could find a pool big enough!

It would be a bad idea to try and land on Uranus. Like the other gas giants, it's a big ball of gas.

Neptune's wild winds can travel faster than a fighter jet!

Neptune

Uranus

Comets and asteroids

Halley's Comet

Our solar system also contains **comets** and **asteroids**. Asteroids are rocky lumps, whereas comets are made up of ice and dust. Both asteroids and comets travel around the **Sun**.

Mad about comets and asteroids

When they pass close to the Sun, comets get hot and leave a trail of gas, which looks like a tail.

The most famous comet is Halley's Comet. It can only be seen from Earth once every 75 years!

Rocky metal

Some **asteroids** are all **rock**, others are all **metal**, but many are a mix of rock and metal.

Thousands of asteroids make up a giant ring between Mars and Jupiter, known as the "asteroid belt."

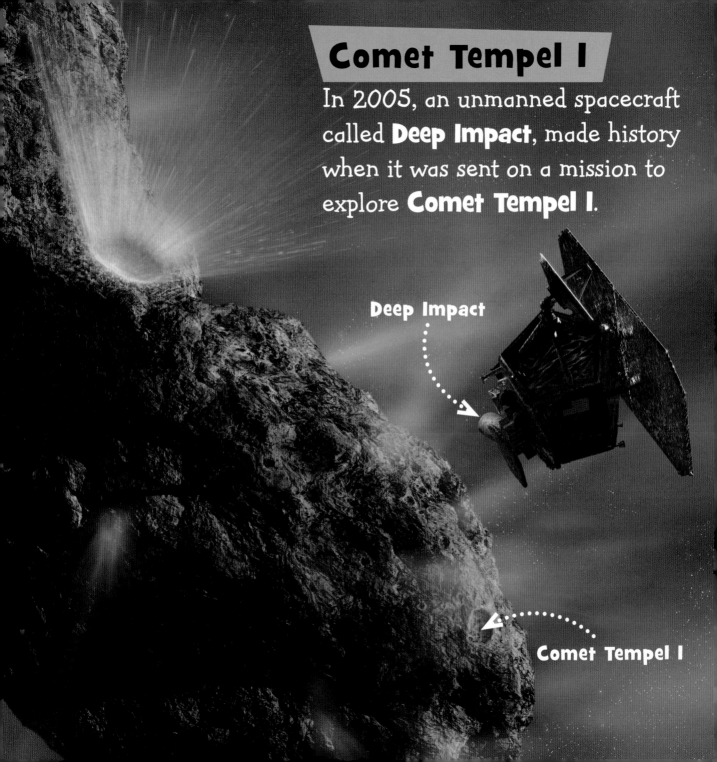

Comet Tempel 1

In 2005, an unmanned spacecraft called **Deep Impact**, made history when it was sent on a mission to explore **Comet Tempel 1**.

Deep Impact

Comet Tempel 1

The Moon

In July 1969, a giant **rocket** called Apollo 11 took off on a journey to the **Moon**. A part of the rocket called the **lunar module** landed on the Moon, with two **astronauts** inside.

back pack

boots......

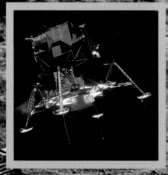

lunar module

Mad about the Moon

Only one side of the Moon can be seen from the Earth. You'd have to go into space to see the other side!

The Moon shines because it reflects some of the sunlight that falls on it. So moonlight is actually sunlight!

If you visit the Kennedy Space Center in America, you can touch a piece of moon rock kept in a special box.

The first astronauts to land on the Moon were American, so they placed an American flag on its surface.

flag

footprint

Craters

The **Moon** is covered with holes called **craters** that were made by collisions with huge rocks. They make the Moon look like a big ball of cheese!

International Space Station

The **International Space Station** is a big spacecraft that circles around the **Earth**. It has been built with the help of many nations to improve our knowledge of space.

Mad about the space station

The station travels nearly 80 times faster than a racing car. It takes just 90 minutes to go around the Earth!

Gravity is the pull that keeps our feet on the ground. Because there is no gravity, toilets on the space station are like big fan-powered vacuum cleaners!

Astronauts have to attach themselves to seats or bunk beds, so they don't float around when they sleep.

The Shuttle

The space **shuttle** takes astronauts and equipment up to the **space station**.

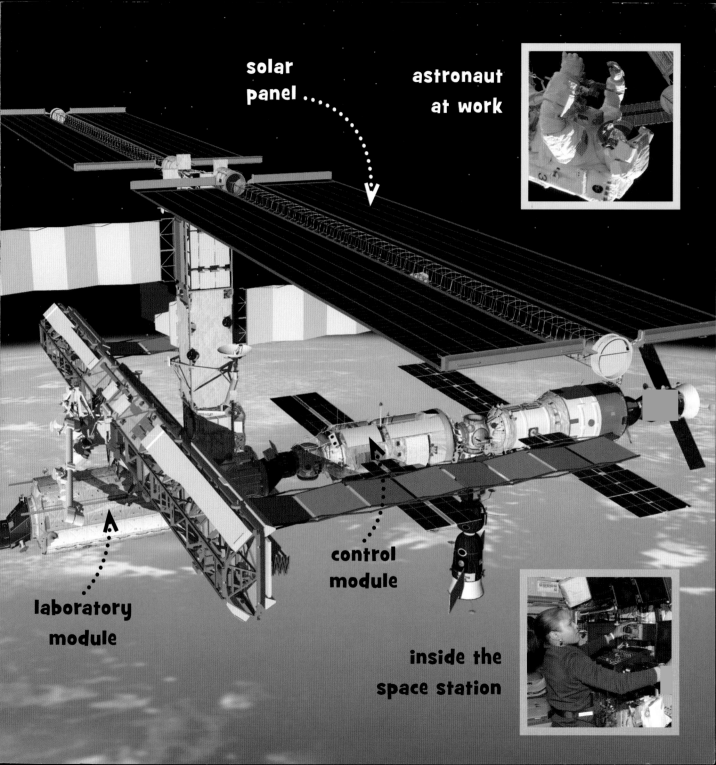

solar panel

astronaut at work

control module

laboratory module

inside the space station

Guess who?

Look at the pictures, read the clues, and guess what each one is.

1
I produce heat and light. I am at the center of the solar system.

2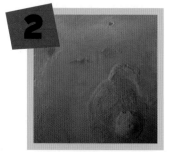
It would take over 66 years to drive to me. I am a rocky planet.

3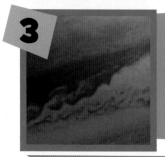
I am the biggest planet in the solar system. I am a gas giant.

4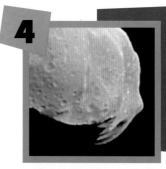
I am a large lump of rock. I travel around the Sun.

5
It takes me just 90 minutes to travel around the Earth!

6
I take astronauts and equipment up to the Space Station.

Answers: 1:the Sun, 2:Mars, 3:Jupiter, 4:an asteroid, 5:The Space Station, 6:the space shuttle.

Picture credits Cover: NASA S84-27017; Our galaxy L:Barney Magrath HYPERLINK "http://www.HawaiiAstronomyArt.com" http://www.HawaiiAstronomyArt.com, R: NASA/JPL-Caltech; The Sun R: SOHO-EIT 304A; Rocky planets BL: NASA Lunar and Planetary Institute, BM: NASA/JPL/GSFC, TL: NASA/John Hopkins University Applied Physics Laboratory/Carnegie Institution of Washington, TM: NASA/JPL, TR: NASA/JPL-Caltech/University of Arizona; Gas planets: BL: NASA/JPL/University of Arizona, BM: NASA Lunar and Planetary Institute, BR: NASA/JPL, TM: NASA/JPL, TR: NASA/JPL/University of Colorado; Comets and asteroids: BL: NASA Solarsystem Collection Asteroid Ida, R: NASA/JPL/UMD; The Moon: BL: NASA AS11-44-6581, M: NASA AS11-40-5903, BM: NASA/JPL/USGS, TR: NASA AS11-40-5875, TM: NASA AS11-40-5877; International Space Station B: NASA MSFC-75-SA-4105-2C, R: NASA JSC2004-E-18457, TR: NASA ISS014-E-10063, BR: NASA ISS014-E-09631; Guess who? 1:SOHO-EIT 304A, 2: NASA/JPL-Caltech/University of Arizona, 4: NASA Solarsystem Collection Asteroid Ida, 5: NASA JSC2004-E-18457, 6: NASA MSFC-75-SA-4105-2C; Sticker pages: As previous.